This book is the winner of the children's story contest by Inclusive Works.

In an effort to create an inclusive society in which everyone can and wants to participate in an equal way, Inclusive Works advises organizations, executes projects, and conducts research on the themes of discrimination, diversity, migration, inclusion, and integration. The Big Five illustrates the positive role that older people play in a child's life from care and education to transferring knowledge and traditions.

For Andile and Thando - B.M.

Copyright © 2019 Clavis Publishing Inc., New York

Originally published as *De grote vijf* in Belgium and Holland by Clavis Uitgeverij, Hasselt–Amsterdam, 2018
English translation from the Dutch by Clavis Publishing Inc., New York

Visit us on the Web at www.clavis-publishing.com.

The Big Five written by Bella Makatini and illustrated by Judi Abbot

ISBN 978-1-60537-457-4 (hardcover edition)
ISBN 978-1-60537-476-5 (softcover edition)

This book was printed in April 2019 at Nikara, M. R. Štefánika 858/25, 963 01 Krupina, Slovakia.

First Edition
10 9 8 7 6 5 4 3 2 1

THE BIG FIVE

Written by Bella Makatini
Illustrated by Judi Abbot

Clavis
NEW YORK

Danny is staying with his grandpa for five days.
He loves to look at Grandpa's beautiful paintings
and colorful masks.
His favorite is a painting of five animals from Africa.

"Those are **the big five**," says Grandpa,
"the most famous animals from my homeland.
Why don't I tell you about one animal each day?"

On Monday, Danny and Grandpa walk to the supermarket.
It's raining, so Danny wears his raincoat and boots.
"What is the **first animal**?" Danny asks Grandpa.
"The first animal is so big that you can see him
from a great distance," says Grandpa.
"He has *big ears*, *big tusks*, and a *long trunk*."

"I know which animal that is," calls Danny. "That's the **elephant**!"
"Very good," says Grandpa.
"And do you know what an elephant is good at? *Stomping!*"
"I can do that too," says Danny. He stomps with his boots in a puddle.
Grandpa stomps with him.

On Tuesday, Danny and Grandpa are making crafts.
Danny uses two toilet paper rolls to make binoculars.
"What is the **second animal**?" he asks.
"The second animal *roars* so *loud* that you can hear him
from a distance," says Grandpa.
"He has a *long mane*, *sharp teeth*, and *dangerous claws*."

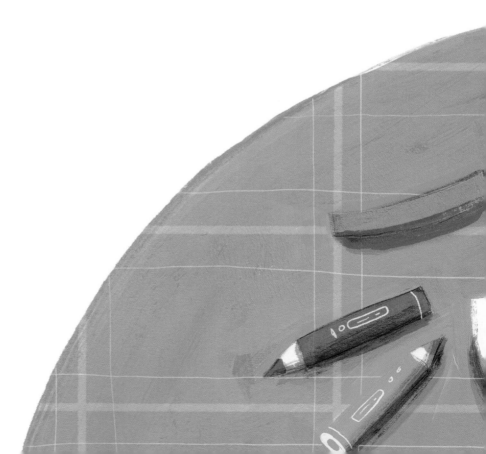

"I know which animal that is," calls Danny. "That's the **lion**!"
"Very good," says Grandpa. "Do you know what a lion is good at? *Jumping!*"
"I can do that too," says Danny. He jumps as far as he can.
Grandpa jumps with him.

On Wednesday, Danny and Grandpa enjoy a picnic in the park.
There are three slices of cucumber left on Danny's plate.
"What is the **third animal**?" he asks.
"The third animal has *thick skin* and *two horns*
on his nose," says Grandpa.

Danny thinks. "That's the **rhino**!"

"Very good," says Grandpa.

"Do you know what a rhino is good at? *Grazing!*"

"I can do that too," says Danny.

He puts a slice of cucumber in his mouth.

Grandpa takes one too.

On Thursday, Danny and Grandpa ride
to the playground.
Danny sits on the back of the bike.
"What is the **fourth animal**?" he asks.
"The fourth animal *looks like a big cat*," says Grandpa.
"He has *soft fur* and is covered with *spots*."

Danny thinks. "That's the **leopard**!"
"Very good," says Grandpa.
"Do you know what a leopard is good at? *Climbing!*"
"I can do that too," says Danny. Danny climbs to the top of the slide.
Grandpa waits for him at the bottom.

Friday is Danny's last day
with Grandpa. Danny plays with
some friends in the yard.
"What is the **fifth animal**?" he asks.
"The fifth animal has *two crooked horns*
above his ears and likes to be with his friends."

Danny isn't sure what animal Grandpa means.
His friends don't know either.
"That's the **buffalo**," says Grandpa.
"And do you know what a buffalo is also good at? *Running!*"
"We can do that too," says Danny.
Danny runs across the yard.
His friends run too.

That night Grandpa has a surprise.
He takes the painting of **the big five** from the wall and gives it to Danny.
"You may take this painting home with you. And when you're bigger,
we'll visit the land where I come from together."
"Wow," says Danny. "Thank you, Grandpa. I can't wait!"